For Jane & David,
Enjoy!
Mitch

LITTLE RED UTE
AND THE UTE PARADE

**For Aaron and Peri, the reddest ute
and the greenest wheelbarrow – M.L.**

For Gabrielle and Aidan – N.Z.

Omnibus Books
335 Unley Road, Malvern SA 5061
an imprint of Scholastic Australia Pty Ltd (ABN 11 000 614 577)
PO Box 579, Gosford NSW 2250.
www.scholastic.com.au

Part of the Scholastic Group
Sydney • Auckland • New York • Toronto • London • Mexico City •
New Delhi • Hong Kong • Buenos Aires • Puerto Rico

First published in 2010.
Text copyright © Mitch Lewis, 2010.
Illustrations copyright © Nahum Ziersch, 2010.

National Library of Australia Cataloguing-in-Publication entry

Author: Lewis, Mitch.
Title: Little Red Ute and the Ute Parade/Mitch Lewis; illustrator Nahum Ziersch
ISBN: 978 1 86291 879 5
Series: Lewis, Mitch. Little Red Ute books; 4.
Target Audience: For preschool age.
Subjects: Sport utility vehicles – Juvenile fiction. Parades – Juvenile fiction.
Other Authors/Contributors: Ziersch, Nahum.
Dewey Number: A823.4

Typeset in Minion Pro.
Printed in China by Toppan Leefung Printing Ltd.

10 9 8 7 6 5 4 3 2 1   10 11 12 13 14 15/ 0

LITTLE RED UTE

AND THE UTE PARADE

Written by **Mitch Lewis**
Illustrated by **Nahum Ziersch**

An Omnibus Book from Scholastic Australia

The foreman wiped the final speck of dust from
Little Red Ute's bonnet.

'All done,' he said, standing back to admire his work.
'Now you're ready for the ute show.'

'What about Green Wheelbarrow?' asked Little Red Ute.

'We can't forget him,' laughed the foreman, wiping Green Wheelbarrow clean.

This was Little Red Ute's first show and he was very excited.

The streets were packed with utes of all shapes and colours.

A black ute rumbled by, riding low to the ground.

Another had a huge dragon
painted along his tray

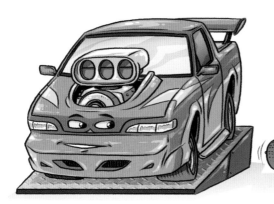

and some had engines so big
they stuck out of their bonnets.

Little Red Ute laughed at the big machine resting under the shade of a tree.

'He looks like a bus,' said Little Red Ute.

'He was a minibus,' said the foreman. 'But now he's a ute, just like you.'

Little Red Ute and Green Wheelbarrow admired a huge bunch of balloons while the foreman headed for a big striped tent.

He returned with a sticker, which he slapped on Little Red Ute's door.

'What's this?' asked Little Red Ute.

'It's your number for the big ute parade,' said the foreman.

'What about Green Wheelbarrow?' asked Little Red Ute.

'Sorry,' said the foreman. 'The parade is only for utes.'

'I wish I was a ute,' said Green Wheelbarrow sadly.
'Then I could have a sticker and enter the parade too.'

'I'm sorry,' said Little Red Ute. 'Maybe one day
there'll be a wheelbarrow parade.'

Soon the announcer called for all utes to gather for the parade.

'Are you coming?' said Little Red Ute excitedly, forgetting Green Wheelbarrow couldn't enter the parade.

'No,' said Green Wheelbarrow quietly. 'Good luck.'

Little Red Ute rolled over to join the other utes.

'Number thirty?' shouted the announcer over the roar and hum of the huge engines. 'Where's number thirty?'

Little Red Ute stuck his aerial in the air.

'Hurry up,' said the announcer. 'Move into position!'

THE UTE PARADE

Little Red Ute moved into his place between a brash new model and a tiny mini ute.

The crowd lined the streets ahead but Little Red Ute's headlights were dim.

'What's wrong?' asked the foreman. 'You've been waiting for this all week.'

'I know,' said Little Red Ute. 'But it isn't the same without Green Wheelbarrow.'

'Okay,' said the foreman, motioning to the announcer. 'Let me see what I can do.'

Little Red Ute felt a thump in his tray.

'It's me!' chirped Green Wheelbarrow. 'Let's go!
The crowd is waiting.'

The people stared in awe at the monster utes, laughed at the minibus and waved to Green Wheelbarrow, who stood on his handlebars and spun his shiny wheel in return.

Little Red Ute winked to the crowd but he saved an extra flash of his headlights for the foreman.

'This was the best parade yet,' said the announcer.

The black low-rider won Gruntiest Ute and the dragon ute won Best Paint Job.

The minibus won Best Conversion but the biggest cheer was saved for the winners of Best Team – Little Red Ute and Green Wheelbarrow.